Cloughwood Ac

Computer Science & ICT Department Library

In
tha

by George N" #

THOMSON

NELSON

Australia · Canada · Mexico · Singapore · Spain · United Kingdom · United States

THOMSON

™

NELSON

Zebras are published by Thomson Learning Australia
and are distributed as follows:

AUSTRALIA
Thomson Learning Australia
Level 7, 80 Dorcas Street
South Melbourne 3205
Victoria

NEW ZEALAND
Unit 4B, Rosedale Office Park
331 Rosedale Road
Albany, North Shore 0632

First published in 2002
10 9 8 7 6 5 4
10 09 08 07

Text © black dog books 2002
Messy Desks
ISBN 978 0 17010742 6
ISBN 978 0 17010846 1 Zebras Set B

a black dog (Australia) book

Designed by Guy Holt Design
Photographs on pp. i, 1, 2, 7, 12, 14, 15, 18, 19,
20, 25, 26, 27 and cover by Fotograffiti
Illustrations on pp. 3, 4, 5, 6, 8, 10, 11, 16, 17, 22 by Rob Mancini
Illustrations on pp. 7, 21, 23, 24 by Guy Holt Design

Teacher consultant: Garry Chapman, Ivanhoe Grammar School

Printed in China by 1010 Printing International Ltd

This title is published under the imprint of Nelson School.
Nelson Australia Pty Limited ACN 058 280 149
(incorporated in Victoria) trading as Thomson Learning Australia.

Contents

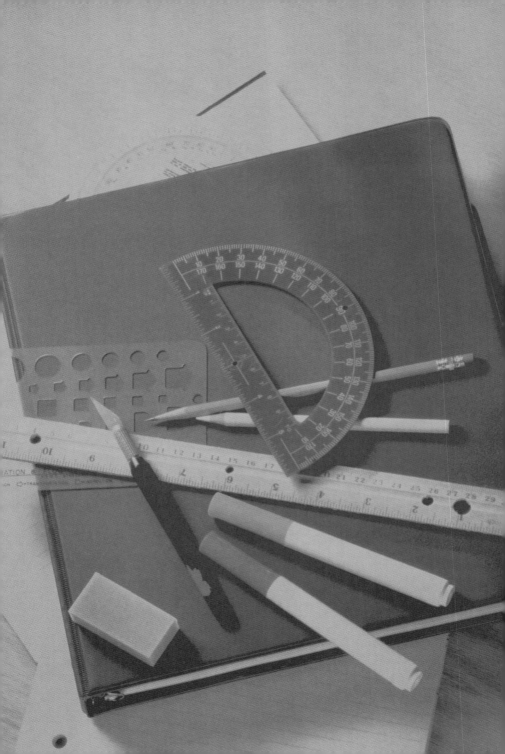

Chapter One

What's On Your Desk?

What do you have on your messy desk? Probably lots of ordinary things. But did you know ordinary things can have extraordinary beginnings?

Let's start with that piece of paper you're writing on.

Paper. You can write on it, draw on it or even make paper aeroplanes with it. But what if you didn't have any paper? There was no paper until the year 150 **CE**. So what did people use before then?

2

Before paper, people used rocks or cave walls. Sometimes they used slabs of wet clay that couldn't be moved until the slabs were dry. Around 2500 **BCE**, people began using parchment, which was made from dried animal skins.

Hieroglyphics means 'writing of the gods'. The Egyptians had a basic alphabet of 24 signs that stood for separate letters, much like the alphabet we have today.

The first writing recorded is not like today's writing. It looked more like small drawings, known today as 'pictographs'.

Over 4,000 years ago, the Egyptians invented one of the first kinds of alphabet, called hieroglyphics (say *hi-ro-glif-icks*). Hieroglyphics looked like pictures, but they were signs for objects and sounds.

4

Chapter Two

Write On!

So, what did people write or draw with before pens were **invented**? Paint made from dirt was a real favourite. People also carved marks into clay or wood. Some people cut their own writing tools from **papyrus** (say *pa-pie-russ*) reed.

In the 1600s, people used the quill (say *kwill*) to write with. The quill was a large feather, often from a goose. It was sharpened and dipped in ink.

By the beginning of the 1800s, a steel **nib** had been added to the quill. This gave it a very fine point. Writing with ink this way was a messy business.

ballpoint pen

ink tube

metal ball

The first practical fountain pen was invented in 1884. Many new improvements have been made since.

It wasn't until recent times that Ladislo Biro invented a pen that used quick-drying ink. His pen had a tiny metal ball rotating at the bottom of a tube full of ink. The ball rolled the ink onto the paper.

Ladislo and his brother Georg made the
first ballpoint pens in 1943. It was wartime
and the 'biros' were popular with soldiers and
pilots because they could write clearly, even
on the battlefield or while flying in planes.

Chapter Three

You Can Count On It

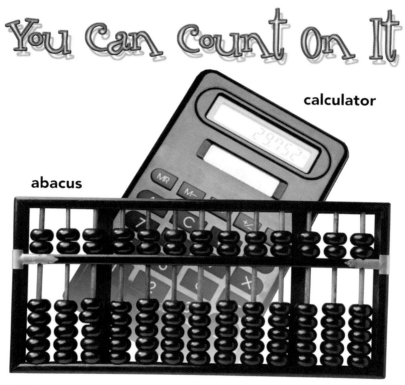

calculator

abacus

Today we use calculators and computers to help us with our work. Long before calculators or computers, the Chinese invented a frame with beads on wire to help them with their maths. It was called an abacus (say *ab-a-kus*), and it is believed to have been around since 3000 BCE.

The Qwerty keyboard got its name from the top line of letters on the first typewriter. The first six letters spell Qwerty!

The typewriter was invented by Sholes and Glidden, and it had a Qwerty keyboard. When typewriters were first sold to the public in 1874, they were an exciting invention. They helped people create words much faster than just writing by hand.

10

ENIAC stands for Electrical Numerical Integrator and Computer. It cost the USA Army $500,000 to build in 1946. The first task of ENIAC was to compute whether or not it was possible to build a hydrogen bomb. After six weeks of thinking, the machine's answer was 'yes'.

Today, most people use a computer instead of a typewriter to create typed words. The first computer was built in the 1940s. It was so big, it filled a whole room and weighed over 30 tonnes. Try fitting that on your messy desk!

Since that first invention, computers have been getting smaller and smaller. We now have personal computers that fit on desks, laptop computers that fit on laps, and small computers that fit into your hand.

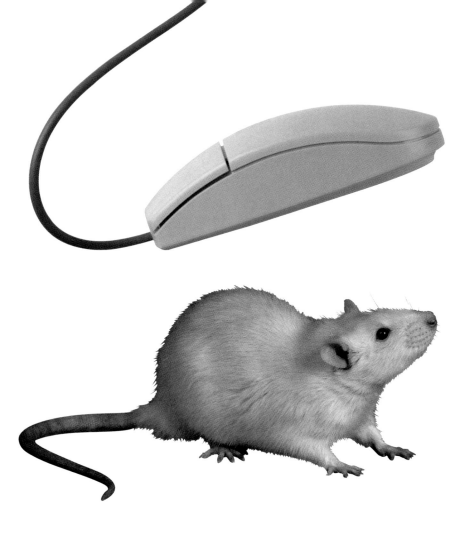

Most desktop computers today come with a mouse as well as a keyboard. The mouse got its name because it originally had two buttons that looked like eyes, and a cord that looked like a tail. It was even shaped like a mouse.

New technology is being invented all the time. Maybe one day, computers will be built straight into your desk. Imagine sitting down at your keyboard and saying, "Computer on!" Then watching as a screen pops up from your desktop!

Chapter Four

Bright Ideas

Many people spend a lot of time working at desks. Perhaps that's why so many inventions have been created for desks. Some have become so popular that we couldn't live without them.

One of the earliest kinds of sticky tape
was invented in the late 1600s. Tiny strips
of paper were wet with glue and used to
make musical instruments. In 1937,
Sellotape was invented.

In 1876, Alexander Graham Bell invented one of the first telephones. At that time, talking over electric lines seemed like a crazy idea. The telephone was originally called an 'electrical speech machine'.

These iridescent blue and black butterflies fly high above the rainforest canopy, landing in clearings to feed for only a few seconds on each flower. when resting with wings closed, the dull coloured underside of the wings helps to camouflage this large butterfly.

I'm a Ulysses and I'm a postcard too!

In 1899, Johan Vaaler invented the paper clip to help keep paper together and tidy. Because he didn't get a **patent** for the paper clip, he didn't get the sole rights to make his invention.

Do you have a handy reminder note stuck on your messy desk? In 1968, Dr Silver invented a type of glue. Unfortunately for Dr Silver, it didn't stick very well.

Fortunately for us, Dr Silver's friend, Arthur Fry, took the glue and used it to invent Post-It Notes.

In the 1960s, Bette Nesmith Graham
invented Liquid Paper to hide the mistakes
she made as a typist. Liquid Paper was
originally called 'Mistake Out'.

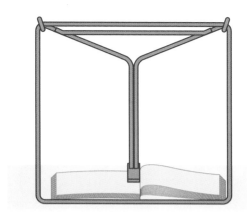

Do you think this invention would help you sit up straight?

Have you ever been told to sit up straight when working at your desk? Way back in 1906, this often happened to Mr Fichtler. To help people sit up straight, he invented a device that stopped them holding their heads too low while reading or writing.

In the USA, Anthony Vandenburg invented a computerised lolly **dispenser**. To use it, you have to connect it to your computer. Every time you answer a question correctly on your computer, you get a lolly. Cool!

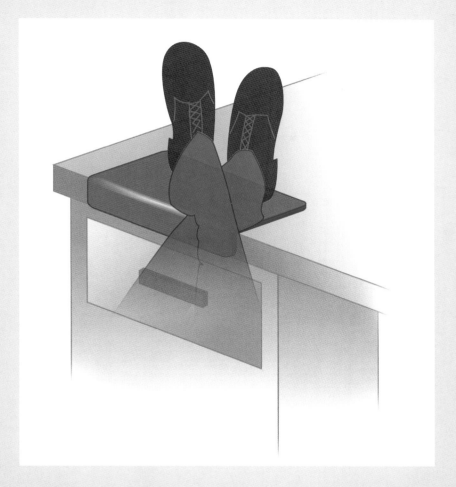

Have you ever seen someone with their feet up on their desk? Maybe they had their shoes on a special L-shaped plastic desk mat to stop damaging their desktop.

Paul J. Glickman filed his patent for this invention in 1974.

If you're thinking about getting a new desk, think about this. One inventor has made a new type of desk that you don't sit at. You lie down to use it! Just be careful not to fall asleep doing your homework.

Chapter Five

InVent It Yourself

Many things have been invented for desks over the years. Inventions can save time, make work easier or they can be just plain fun. Anyone with an imagination can be an inventor.

Perhaps you'd like to be an inventor. Do you ever chew on the end of your pen? Not very tasty! Could you come up with an idea to make it taste better? That would be a great invention.

Next time you sit down at your messy desk, think about what could help make your job easier. Maybe you could invent something to turn your messy desk into a tidy one!

Glossary

BCE before the Common Era.
CE the Common Era.
dispenser something that gives out things.
invented something that has been created or designed for the first time.
nib the pointed end part of a pen.
papyrus (say *pa-pie-russ*) material made from a water plant.
patent gives a person the sole right to make his or her invention.

Index